A *Callahan* CAROL

A *Callahan* CAROL

A BRAZOS BEND HOLIDAY NOVELLA

Emily March

A Callahan Carol is a work of fiction. Names, characters, places, and incidents are the products of the author's imagination or are used fictitiously. Any resemblance to actual events, locales, or persons, living or dead, is entirely coincidental.

Copyright © 2010, 2014 by Geralyn Dawson Williams.
All rights reserved.

Published in the United States by Emily March Books.

ISBN 13: 9781942002123
ISBN 10: 1942002122

FORWARD

A Summary of Prior Events

Once upon a time following years of infertility, the beloved wife of Texas oilman and rancher Branch Callahan gave birth to a son. A religious woman, Margaret Mary named her child for the apostle Matthew. Life in Brazos Bend was good.

The following year, the Callahan marriage again was blessed, this time with identical twin boys, Mark and Luke. Four years later, Branch and Margaret Mary welcomed yet another son. He was given the name John and he was treasured by all.

The Callahan family lived, loved and thrived in their small, Texas Hill Country town. As children, the mischievous boys earned the nickname Holy Terrors, but they were good boys at heart and the townspeople tolerated their hijinks.

Sadly, when the boys were in their teens, tragedy struck the family. Margaret Mary sickened and died.

Branch sank into mourning so dark, deep and powerful that he neglected his sons completely. In this way, the Callahan brothers lost both their mother and their father.

The boys dealt with their own intense grief by elevating mischief-making to recklessness. Their bad behavior culminated one night in an act of drunken carelessness that burned a local factory—the town's largest employer—to the ground.

In the aftermath, an angry and bitter Branch Callahan banished his boys from Brazos Bend.

Years passed. The boys grew to men—fine men. Matt's calling took him into clandestine service with the CIA. Mark found his place as a Military Intelligence investigator. Luke worked undercover for the DEA. John's talent for languages took him to the State Department. As adults, the Callahan brothers reconnected and moved toward reconciliation with their father—until tragedy struck the family once again.

John was attacked, kidnapped, and held for ransom by Eastern European criminals. Branch's misguided efforts to secure his release failed. The Callahans learned that their beloved son and brother had perished. The family broke.

A Callahan Carol

More years passed. The surviving sons remained estranged from their father until, one by one, exceptional women entered—or, in Mark's case, reentered—the lives of the Callahan men. First, Luke met Maddie Kincaid, aka Baby Dagger, the infamous rocker love child who helped mend the fence between father and son. Then Matt tangled with Torie Bradshaw and loving her precipitated his reconciliation with Branch. Finally, the healing of Mark's damaged relationship with his ex, Annabelle Monroe, allowed forgiveness to enter his heart.

Then, on the occasion of Mark and Annabelle's second wedding, they and the rest of the Callahan family received a priceless gift from an old enemy: news that John was alive.

The Callahans were ecstatic. Each of them reached out to contacts all over the world trying to locate him. Months dragged by, then years. Despite vigorous and intensive searches, the Callahans failed to discover even a sliver of evidence to indicate that John had, indeed, survived.

Was it just a vicious lie? Another wound inflicted by the cruelest of enemies? Privately, Mark began to wonder. Lying awake in bed in the middle of the night, Luke despaired. Each time he held his young son, Johnny, Matt fought back fears that the boy's namesake was indeed long departed from this earth.

Branch Callahan, the aging but still stubborn patriarch of the Callahan family, remained convinced that one day John Gabriel Callahan would walk through the front door of Callahan House, the family home in Brazos Bend.

But even a man as strong as Branch had his limits. Finally, on yet another anniversary of John's birth and faced with yet another milestone that tore his heart in two, the months and years of futile searching finally defeated him. Branch lost his faith, his hope, and his love.

Branch Callahan became the Scrooge of Brazos Bend.

PART ONE

Brazos Bend, Texas

"I can't believe Grandpa Branch wants to cancel Christmas," seven-year-old Johnny Callahan declared as he hopped down from the cab of his father's pickup on a clear, crisp December morning. He kicked a brittle leaf from a cottonwood tree that lay in the driveway of his grandfather's house as he waited for his father to open the built-in tool box on his truck.

Johnny's cousin, nine-year-old Samantha, put her hands on her hips and frowned at the facade of the Callahan House. "Grandpa Branch is very sad. My mama says he's lost his belief in miracles because no one has been able to find Uncle John. Christmas is all about miracles."

Johnny spied a big black beetle crossing the driveway. He ran to it and squashed it with his sneaker. "My mom says he'll be really mad when he gets home and sees that we've decorated the house and put up the Wonderland."

"My mom says the same thing." Samantha tucked a strand of curly red hair behind her ear as she stood patiently beside the truck.

"Your mothers are brilliant women," said Johnny's dad, Matt Callahan. He handed child-sized leather tool belts to his son and niece.

"So...why are we trying to make Grandpa Branch mad?" Johnny asked as he buckled the belt around his waist.

Dad gazed out over the lawn. "We're not trying to make him angry, but he can't cancel Christmas; not the Callahan Wonderland display, anyway. It's a beloved tradition in this town. It's important to our friends and neighbors."

Samantha's freckled nose bobbed up and down as she nodded. "Mrs. Branson told my mom that it wouldn't be Christmas without a visit to the Wonderland."

"I know I would miss it." Johnny followed his father's gaze out over the huge, empty lawn at Callahan House and imagined how it would look at the end of the day after all of their work. He thought the Wonderland was the coolest thing ever. "Did you love the Wonderland when you were a boy, Dad?"

"Absolutely. I still love it."

"Me, too!" Samantha said.

"Me, three!" Johnny agreed, then added, "I wonder if Stinkweed will love it four."

"Better not let your mom hear you calling your sister that again, Johnny," Dad cautioned. The toddler's real name was Sophie. Johnny's parents had adopted her the previous fall after the girl's parents died in a plane crash.

"She calls her Buttercup," Johnny protested. "That's just as mean."

His dad shook his head. "You have a lot to learn, boyo. Now, are y'all ready to get to work?"

Samantha nodded and Johnny called out, "I'm ready!"

To illustrate, he pulled the kid-sized hammer out of its loop and smashed a pecan lying at the edge of the driveway, then he kicked it into the grass in just about the spot where they would put Santa's workshop. "Dibs on putting Santa's feet in the bucket."

Samantha folded her arms and scowled. "Hey, no fair! You did it last year."

Dad frowned at Johnny over the top of his sunglasses. "Your cousin is right. It's her turn."

Johnny sighed. Darn. He'd hoped they wouldn't remember. Putting Santa's tired feet in the bucket of the Santa's Workshop display was the final step in setting up the Wonderland, sort of like putting the star on the top of the Christmas tree. Like putting sprinkles on top of Mama's sugar cookies. It was special.

Oh, well. Johnny shrugged off the disappointment. The whole day was special.

Excitement added a skip to his step as he followed his dad toward the storage building in the backyard. The Callahan Christmas Wonderland yard decorations were the oldest, the biggest, and the best in Brazos Bend. Maybe even the best in the whole state. Johnny's great-grandmother had started the collection back in the 1930's; his grandmother had continued the tradition and added to it. Now when it was all set up the displays filled the entire yard—and Grandpa Branch's yard was humongous.

People drove from all over the county to see the Wonderland at Callahan House at Christmas. Samantha's twin sister Catherine said that people even drove over from Fort Worth to see the show. Johnny didn't know if he believed that—Catherine told stories a lot—but cars did line up for blocks.

The hinges on the Christmas storage shed squeaked loudly as his dad opened the door. Johnny peeked inside, then gasped with delight at his first sight of the bubble robot. Next to the Santa's Workshop grand finale decoration, the bubble-blowing robot was his absolute favorite.

His dad handed a coil of yellow extension cord to him and a plastic tub full of twinkle lights to Samantha. "All right, you two. You know the drill."

"Yes, sir, Uncle Matt." Sam saluted her uncle, then picked up the bin and toted it toward the front yard. Johnny looped the cord around his shoulder and followed.

Johnny had made three trips between the shed and the front yard when another pickup rolled to the curb and parked. The doors opened. Two men climbed out. Both wore jeans and flannel shirts and looked so much alike that, as usual, Johnny had trouble telling them apart.

The truck was Uncle Luke's so he guessed that the driver, wearing the blue shirt, must be him. The uncle in the red shirt waved and said, "Hey, Chip. What's with the empty yard? I thought you were going to have all the work done before we got here."

Now, Johnny was sure which uncle was which. Uncle Mark was the one who liked to call him Chip (as in chip off the old block). "You know what Dad says, Uncle Mark. That's what you get for thinking."

"Where's your cousin?" Uncle Luke held up a purple TCU Horned Frogs windbreaker. "Her mom sent a jacket for her."

"Here I am, Daddy." Samantha came around the corner of the house with another box of lights. "I don't need a jacket."

He tossed her the windbreaker. "Put it on anyway so I don't get into trouble."

With the arrival of his uncles, work began in earnest. Soon the Old Woman in the Shoe display had joined the Bubble Robot, along with the Gingerbread House and Snow White and the Seven Dwarves. When the Christmas shed was empty, Johnny's dad made a phone call and within minutes the work crew from Brazos Bend Electric Co-op arrived. Next, the big truck from

Brazos Bend Storage showed up to deliver the displays that were too big to fit in the Christmas shed.

While the crew unloaded the truck and the head electrician directed the installation, Dad and Uncle Luke went to work stringing lights on Grandpa Branch's house. The kids helped Uncle Mark place the lights on the bushes. With the setting of every spotlight, the connection of each new string of lights, Johnny's excitement grew. It was hard but exciting work. Within hours they'd turned Callahan House into the familiar–and magical–Callahan Christmas Wonderland.

Johnny was so proud he'd been born a Callahan.

"What time is the Christmas play rehearsal at church supposed to be over?" he asked Sam as they ate peanut butter sandwiches for lunch.

"Not until 1:00," she replied, swiping at a smear of grape jam with the back of her hand. "I'm so glad Mom isn't making me do that this year. I always had to be a shepherd."

Johnny wasn't in the play this year, either. Being on stage made him feel like throwing up, so Dad said he didn't have to do it anymore. He glanced at the clock. "I hope they get here pretty soon. I heard my mom tell your mom that we'd better have everything done before Grandpa Branch comes home."

At 1:20, Johnny's mother and aunts arrived with more of his cousins—Catherine, their little sister Savannah, and Uncle Mark's kids, Emma and Tanner. Uncle Mark's son Chris was grown up and he'd taken Grandpa Branch to the Dallas Cowboy football game, which was why the family had been able to assemble the Wonderland without interference.

The family worked together to put the finishing touches on the Wonderland, and they all gathered around when Samantha put Santa's feet in the bucket. The moms clapped and the kids cheered and the dads whistled, then everyone headed inside where the women took charge of decorating. Aunt Maddie hung the Christmas stockings, Aunt Annabelle put up the wreaths, and Johnny's Mom wrapped a fresh evergreen garland around the banister of the staircase. Callahan House began to smell like Christmas.

Then it was time to tackle the tree.

Johnny heard his mother tell Uncle Luke, "No telling what we're going to find in the library. I almost wish Mark wasn't so handy picking locks."

"Hey now, Red," Luke protested. "I'm just as good as Mark."

"Neither of you are as good as me," Johnny's dad declared.

Aunt Maddie and Mom rolled their eyes. Aunt Annabelle sighed and said, "Somebody open the door, would you, please? We don't have a lot of time. Chris called an hour ago to give me a heads up that the Cowboys game had ended. He'll be back with Branch by five."

The three brothers looked at one another, then Dad said, "Luke, you've always been the fastest. Go ahead."

"The Callahan men's talents continue to amaze me," Aunt Maddie said when the door swung open minutes later.

"So does their stubbornness," Mom added.

"And Branch is the king of stubborn." Aunt Annabelle shook her head. "If I ever had any doubts, this latest nonsense with the library would have convinced me. Leaving the Christmas tree up until John came home was a lovely gesture, but if he didn't want it around anymore, he should have had it taken down. Locking Christmas away solved nothing."

"At least it was an artificial tree," Dad observed, following the women into the room.

"Look at the dust in here. We should have picked that lock months ago."

"How long has he left it up?"

"Three years at least," Uncle Mark said.

Uncle Luke added, "Maybe four."

"We could count the presents and see," Cousin Catherine suggested.

Uncle Luke said, "I think it's time to store John's gifts somewhere out of sight."

The aunts and his mom shared a look, then Aunt Annabelle said, "Maybe it's time to—"

"Donate them," Mom finished.

Aunt Maddie added, "To charity."

"No!" snapped all three Callahan men simultaneously. Luke added, "Out of sight is fine. Then let's get our gifts to Branch under the tree."

The family went to work dusting, decorating and sprucing up the artificial spruce standing in a corner of the room. Aunt Annabelle asked Uncle Mark to find a Christmas music station on the radio, and he and Johnny sang along to "Grandma Got Run Over By A Reindeer." In the kitchen, Mom spooned ginger cookie dough onto a metal sheet and slipped it into the oven to bake, while Aunt Maddie heated spiced cider on the stove. Soon the scrumptious scents of ginger and apples and cinnamon filled the air and Johnny's tummy started to growl.

When the cookies were done, the cider hot, and the decorating and cleaning complete, everyone got a snack and went outside. They took their traditional seats on the curb in front of the house across the street while Catherine and Samantha ran up and down the street knocking on the neighbors' front doors and telling them the big moment was finally here. Then, at his mother's signal, Johnny's dad flipped the main switch.

The Callahan Christmas Wonderland came to life.

Lights blazed, the displays moved. The mannequins in choir robes sang. Johnny and his cousins clapped their hands, jumped up and down, and shouted with excitement and delight. The adults all told each other "Merry Christmas" and of course, all of the Callahan men kissed their wives. (They did that *all* the time.)

Cousin Chris's red car turned the corner at the end of the block a few minutes later. "Heads up, everyone," Aunt Maddie called.

Johnny could hear Grandpa Branch's angry roar before the car came to a stop. Uncle Mark said, "Batten down your red noses, reindeers. It's gonna be a bumpy ride."

"Don we now our chain-mail armor," Uncle Luke sang softly to the tune of "Deck the Halls," before continuing, "Maddie? Why don't you be point man on this? You've always been able to twist Branch around your little finger."

"Not hardly," she replied, but she stepped toward the car anyway.

Grandpa Branch threw open the passenger-side door and bellowed, "Christopher, get my damned walker out of the trunk."

"Welcome home, Branch," Aunt Maddie said, pasting a big, friendly smile on her face. "How was the ball game? Did the Cowboys win?"

A Callahan Carol

He ignored her question, ignored her, and shot an angry glare toward his sons. "Turn it off. Take it down."

Aunt Maddie sent a "help me" look over her shoulder. Uncle Luke and his brothers moved to stand beside her. "Let's take this inside," Dad said.

"No. I'm going inside. You are gonna take that crap off my damned lawn."

"Watch your language, Branch," Luke demanded. "The kids are here."

Grandpa Branch scowled, yanked his walker from Chris's hands, and shuffled toward his front door. Chris shut his trunk, rubbed the back of his neck, then grimaced. "I tried to soften him up about Christmas on the ride back, but he wasn't hearing anything of it."

"The old goat," Uncle Mark muttered.

"Actually, make that the old Grinch," Dad grumbled.

"He's hurting," Aunt Maddie said, her voice soft.

"Yeah, well, we're all hurting," Uncle Luke replied, just as the first cars full of Wonderland viewers arrived.

Mom sighed and clapped her hands. "Okay, kiddos, looks like the Brazos Bend grapevine has done its job. Santa hats and candy canes are in my back seat. Take your places."

"Do you have any reindeer antlers this year, Aunt Torie?" Uncle Mark's son Tanner asked. "I like wearing antlers better."

Mom ruffled Tanner's hair. "I have a pair of reindeer antlers with your name on it." Then she looked at his dad and uncles and said, "Good luck, you guys."

"We'll need it."

Johnny watched his dad and his brothers follow their father into Callahan House before joining his aunts and cousins in the annual tradition of passing out candy to those who came to view the Wonderland. Cars passed by the house in a steady stream and soon, Johnny's candy bag was empty. Holding it up, he called, "Mom, I'm going for a refill."

She waved at him, then helped Aunt Annabelle's one-year-old hand a peppermint to the neighborhood piano teacher.

After refilling his bag from the supplies in his mother's car, Johnny paused. He needed to pee.

That presented a dilemma. Mom would have a fit if he peed outdoors, but she wouldn't want him going inside, either. After a moment's deliberation (and because he wanted to know what was happening inside) he headed around back toward the kitchen door. As he reached for the knob, he heard Samantha whisper loudly, "Hey, Johnny. Did you come to spy on the grown-ups, too?"

He wasn't about to tell a girl he needed to pee. "Yes."

"I'm worried about Grandpa Branch. He looked really mad."

And really old, Johnny thought. *Really, really old.*

Samantha continued, "Let's go in. But be quiet!"

"You're the one doing all the talking," Johnny grumbled as he carefully turned the knob, then pushed the door open and stepped inside Callahan House. Samantha followed right on his heels.

Now he needed to pee even worse. Doing things he shouldn't always did that to him.

Samantha moved around him to take the lead—as usual. He didn't really mind because if they were caught, she'd catch the worst of it.

They moved into the kitchen. He could hear the sound of raised voices coming from the far side of the house. The sound pulled them forward like a magnet. When they heard Grandpa Branch shout out a curse that would have grounded them for a month, Johnny and Samantha shared a round-eyed look.

"Give me back my gun!" Branch shouted.

"No!" Dad shot back. "You're acting crazy."

"Our kids are outside," Uncle Luke added. "If you want to destroy more than seventy years of family history and tradition so bad, then take a golf club and do it."

Johnny and Samantha crept forward until they stood just outside of the library. The door hung open wide. Samantha dropped down on her hands and knees and peered around the edge, then gestured that it was safe for Johnny to cross to the other side. Holding his breath, he darted past the open doorway. He knelt and mimicked his cousin's stance. Now he really, really, really needed to pee, but the showdown inside the library had him rooted to the spot.

"The Callahan family is more than a Christmas lawn display." Grandpa Branch declared. "Our name is all over this town. Doing away with that nonsense outside won't make any difference at all."

"It'll make a difference to our kids," Uncle Mark fired back, his stance wide, his arms crossed, and his eyes angry.

"And frankly," Dad added, his hands braced on his hips and his jaw jutting forward, "it makes a difference to us, too. The Wonderland is part of our lives. Part of our family and our home. Part of our Christmas."

"He's right." Uncle Luke leaned against one of the floor-to-ceiling bookshelves, his legs crossed at his ankles. His arms where crossed, too, and he looked mad. "Those years when I was away from Brazos Bend for the holidays, I always made the effort to find some sort of Christmas display to visit. It helped me feel…less alone." He shrugged. "Some of them were bigger than ours, but none of them were better. It is important, Branch."

"It's a lie! That's what it is. Think about the buzz words people spout this time of year. Peace on Earth. Joy to the World. It's all bull. There is no peace in Christmas. No joy. Certainly no hope. It's all a lie and be damned if I'll be a part of it any longer."

Johnny's eyes went even rounder when he saw his grandfather reach for his cane and swipe the hooked end toward the Christmas tree.

"I want it *gone!*" Grandpa Branch shouted. "I want it *over!*"

The tree toppled and crashed to the floor. Glass ornaments shattered. Tears stung Johnny's eyes.

Then Grandpa dropped the cane, clutched at his chest, and fell to the floor beside the Christmas tree.

"Faking another heart attack, Dad?" Uncle Mark said. Almost immediately, he repeated in a worried tone, "Dad?"

Uncle Luke said, "I'll call 911."

Johnny's daddy knelt beside Grandpa Branch, placed his fingers against his throat and spoke in a grim tone. "I can't get a pulse."

"He's dead?" Uncle Mark and Uncle Luke asked together.

When his dad didn't say anything else, Johnny Callahan's heart broke.

PART TWO

Coma.

That's what Mom and Dad said was wrong with his grandfather. They used some other big medical words that Johnny couldn't understand or remember, but what really mattered was that Grandpa Branch was asleep and not waking up.

Sixteen days had passed since the ambulance roared up to Callahan House to take him to the hospital, five days since they'd brought him home and installed him in his bedroom because Johnny had overheard Uncle Luke say that Branch would want to die at Callahan House in his own bed.

It had been the worst two weeks Johnny could remember. Mom couldn't seem to stop crying and he'd hardly seen his dad. Branch Callahan's sons all but lived at the hospital. Samantha said that all the grown-ups felt guilty because even though the doctors said otherwise, they thought that decorating for Christmas had brought on the attack.

They hadn't taken down the Wonderland, but the lights stayed off. In the library, the Christmas tree lay on the floor where it had fallen. Nobody felt like cleaning it up. Aunt Maddie had tried to go into the room and clean twice but both times she started crying so hard she had to stop.

In his bedroom, Grandpa Branch lay against dark blue sheets, his face as white as the snow that had begun to fall. Any other time, Johnny would be thrilled to see snow in Brazos Bend, since it had only happened twice before in his whole life that he could remember. Now he didn't care about the snow. Tomorrow was Christmas Eve, and the holiday was shaping up to be the worst Christmas ever.

He sat on the front stoop at Callahan House, watching the neighbor kids making snow angels in the yard across the street. He tried to work up the energy to go play with them but he just didn't have the heart. He sighed heavily, watching his breath fog on the cold winter air, and wishing he still believed in Santa because if he did he would make an emergency trip to the mall and ask old Kris Kringle to bring a get well gift for Grandpa Branch.

The door opened behind him. Samantha came out. Tears slipped down her cheeks. Johnny tensed and swallowed hard. "Is Grandpa…?"

"The doctor just told my dad to…" Her breath caught on a sob. "…to prepare the family. He said Grandpa's body is shutting down."

"What does that mean?"

"He's dying. The doctor said he probably has only a few days left."

Johnny shoved to his feet. His heart pounded with pain. "Well, they need to give him medicine and make it stop."

"That's what I said. Aunt Torie said the doctors have done all they can."

"They need to call different doctors!" he insisted. "Ones who know more."

Tears stung Johnny's eyes as he turned away from his cousin. His gaze landed on the manger scene and he thought about Jesus and the miracle of His birth. Samantha's gaze followed his and a moment later, she murmured, "Maybe that's it."

"What's it?"

"It's the season of miracles, isn't it? Maybe God will give one to Grandpa Branch."

Hope flickered to life inside Johnny. "Maybe He will help us find the right doctor!"

His cousin frowned. "I don't think the grown-ups are going to start looking for new doctors, Johnny. I heard your dad tell mine that Dr. Reed was the best in the business."

"So what will we do?"

Samantha gave the manger scene another long look, her stare fastening on the angels that hung above it. "We'll just have to do the work and find a doctor."

"How are we supposed to do that? We're just kids."

Samantha rolled her eyes. "We'll Google one, of course."

Five minutes later, she sat at the computer in the family room with her hands paused over the keyboard. She entered three words: miracle, healing, and doctor. "Add another word," Johnny said. "It's Christmas."

"I think 'Christmas Miracle' will give us stuff about babies," Samantha said.

"No. Add 'angel.'"

"Oh. Good idea." The search returned 3,400,000 results.

Samantha clicked on the top one. The website loaded. A big Victorian house stood at the base of a forested mountain, a clear mountain creek bubbling in the foreground. "Angel's Rest, Healing Center and Spa," Samantha read. "That sounds good, don't you think?"

"It doesn't look much like a hospital," Johnny said, doubt in his tone.

"We tried a hospital. It didn't work. This says it is a healing center. Grandpa Branch needs healing."

She reached for the phone and dialed the number, then pushed the button to put the call on speaker. After two rings, a woman's voice answered. "Angel's Rest. Celeste Blessing speaking. How may I help you today?"

"My name is Samantha Callahan. My cousin Johnny Callahan is with me. We're from Brazos Bend, Texas. We need a miracle, ma'am."

"A miracle? Two days before Christmas?"

"Yes, ma'am," Johnny said, hope replacing his doubt. Celeste Blessing had a nice voice. The sound of it made him feel warm inside.

"Well, children. I have a feeling that you've come to the right place."

∽

Branch Callahan floated in a misty place. He wasn't dead; he was sure about that. But he wasn't exactly brimming with life, either.

He might be asleep, but he doubted it. He had no sense of the passage of time. At first, he'd believed he was dreaming but that didn't feel right anymore. He had no recall of anything after he'd pulled down the Christmas tree in his library—when? Today? Yesterday? A year ago?

The uncertainty was unsettling.

As was the fact that he couldn't move his body. Not his legs or his feet. Not his arms or his hands. He couldn't roll over or sit up. At least he didn't hurt anywhere for a change. He did have that going for him. Still, he sure would like to wake up. Or die. Dying would be good–unless the redemption he'd been trying to earn the last few years fell short of the mark.

He wished something would happen. Anything.

As soon as the thought formed, he got his wish.

He heard a sound, a rumble that slowly grew louder. Branch attempted to turn toward the sound...and to his surprise, he could do it. He spied a dark shadow in the white-gray mist. The sound intensified. A motor, he identified. A motorcycle? He tried to sit up and this time, his body accommodated him. *Well, what do you know?*

He focused on the shadow, holding his breath, until first a black tire emerged from the mist. It was a motorcycle. A Harley? No, a Honda Gold Wing. Driven by a figure dressed in white leather trimmed in gold and wearing a golden helmet.

Could he be dead, after all? Had Elvis come to drive him off to the Land of Jelly Donuts?

The motor switched off and in the sudden silence, he'd have sworn he heard harp music. The figure heeled down the kickstand, dismounted, pulled off white leather gloves then reached up to remove the helmet.

Not Elvis, Branch thought as a face was revealed, but a woman. A woman of indefinite age.

Her silver-gray hair suggested she was older, but her face remained unlined and her rosy complexion had a youthful glow. She moved her gently-rounded body in a sprightly manner as she advanced toward him and smiled. "Hello, Branch Callahan."

Suddenly, he felt a tingling in his throat and tried to speak. His voice emerged raspy and weak, but he did have a voice. "Who are you? Where am I? What the hell—uh—heck is going on?"

"I'm a...friend of the family. From..." She made sweeping gesture with her hand. "...way back. I have been sent here on a special mission."

"Sent here by whom? My boys?"

"Not exactly. I've been sent by a great and powerful force. A force that–if you allow it–can make an enormous positive impact upon your life. First, however, you must open your heart to it."

"A force?" he asked warily. "What, is this Star Wars? I fell asleep and woke up in a movie?"

She laughed and the sound chimed like church bells.

"What kind of force?" he insisted, suddenly filled with unease. She wasn't carrying a pitchfork and he saw no signs of a pointy tail on her behind, but hey, the Trickster came by that nickname honestly.

"Love. You must open your heart to love, Branch Callahan."

Oh. One of those do-gooders. Branch scowled. "What sort of nonsense is this? I have plenty of love in my heart. I have so much love in my heart that it's killing me."

"Ah. Do you? Or is something else dousing the flame of your love?"

Her smile was beautiful and warm and Branch could feel it deep within his bones. She held out her hand toward him. "Come with me, Branch Callahan. Let me show you the truth."

Suddenly, he was standing—without pain, without needing his walker. He glanced down and noticed he was wearing his own set of leathers, only his were black.

She handed him a black helmet, and then she climbed onto the motorcycle and motioned for Branch to take the passenger position. She started the engine and they took off through the mist. Branch heard "Oh Come All Ye Faithful" piping through the helmet into his ears.

Christmas. Okay, maybe he hadn't drifted as long as he'd thought. Or maybe this entire thing was a dream.

The music segued into "Hark the Herald Angels Sing." Branch frowned. Surely he wasn't having a Jimmy Stewart *It's a Wonderful Life* moment!

Even as the thought formed, the Gold Wing emerged from the mists onto the street in front of Callahan House. The blasted Christmas Wonderland was still up on his lawn, lit up and blasting Christmas cheer all over town, but something about the scene was different. That something bothered him, nagged at him, but he couldn't put his finger on the problem until the front door opened and four little boys burst from within, followed by their mother. That's when he got it. The Christmas Wonderland was missing some of the newer displays and the trees and shrubs around the house were smaller.

Branch swallowed hard. Oh, no. He was already haunted by enough things in life. He didn't need this.

This wasn't a Jimmy Stewart moment. It wasn't even a dream about the Grinch. He wasn't dealing with Clarence the friendly angel or the Who's of Whoville. Gathering in his front yard were the Ghosts of Christmas Past.

Branch's stomach rolled. He was about to be Scrooged.

Two days before Christmas on the second day of the elementary school's holiday break, Margaret Mary Callahan called to her sons. "All right, you little reindeer. If you've run off enough steam and are ready to settle down, the Christmas cookies are ready to be decorated."

"Hooray!" Matt replied.

"Dibs on the red icing," Mark said.

"No fair," Luke protested. "You got to be red last time."

John nodded briskly, his little boy's eyes round and wide. "He's right, Mommy. Remember? Mark put it all over me and said it was blood."

Margaret clicked her tongue. "Yes, I remember. He got into trouble for it, too. This year we're not going to fight over frosting colors. You each have your own set."

"Cool!" Matt darted toward the door. "We can all get bloody."

"The Christmas Spirit is alive and well at the Callahans," Margaret Mary joked.

The children slid into their customary chairs around the kitchen table. For the next hour, with Christmas carols playing softly on the stereo, they labored to turn sugar cookie Christmas trees into works of iced art. Branch came home just as the boys were finishing up the last of the cookies. As his sons competed to offer him first taste of their edible works of art, he stacked the four cookies and did a Cookie Monster impression—by shoving them all into his mouth at once and saying, "Cookies."

The children dissolved into fits of giggles. Margaret sighed, shook her head, then poured him a glass of milk. After Branch washed down the cookies, he asked his family about their day. The older boys told him about the pick-up football game they'd had at the elementary school playground. Margaret Mary relayed a story about the Angel Tree project the church did for the local nursing home. Branch then shared details about his workday, but as soon as he shifted to the subject of mineral rights acquisition, the older boys wandered off.

John hung around. Pretty soon, he crawled into his father's lap. "Would you read me a story, Daddy?"

"Sure. What do you want?"

"The Grinch!" John exclaimed. "He's my favorite!"

"Why is that?" Branch asked his son as if this weren't an exchange they held every single time Branch read the book to the boy.

"Because he reminds me of you."

At that point, as always, Branch attacked with tickles. John giggled, squirmed and giggled some more. When his mother finally handed the beloved book to his father to read, he curled against Branch, stuck his thumb in his mouth, and listened quietly and intently.

When Branch finished, he shut the book and expected John to scramble down and wander away or ask for a second story. Instead, his youngest son remained where he was.

Branch glanced down at John. The boy wasn't asleep. Branch could tell by his expression that something was bothering him. "What's wrong, Buddy?"

Another thirty seconds dragged by before John spoke. "Daddy, Brett Parker said Santa Claus isn't real. I asked my brothers if he was fibbing, but they wouldn't tell. Was he, Daddy? Is Santa Claus just a story?"

Branch sucked in a breath, then put his head up to gaze with wild, worried eyes toward his wife. Santa Claus? What was he supposed to do? This wasn't his job! Margaret took care of the hard stuff with the kids. She handled these sorts of questions. Shoot, she probably knew the complete text of the "Yes, Virginia there is a Santa Claus" letter by heart!

But judging by the sympathetic smile she gave him, she had no intention of handling this one.

Branch gazed down into his son's pleading eyes and sent up a silent prayer. *Just one more year. One more Christmas. Please?*

Quickly, he arrived at a plan. "You don't listen to Brett Parker, John. What you need to know is that I believe in Santa, but I understand how a man can have doubts. Tell you what we will do. I'll put on my thinking cap and try to come up with a way to prove it. Would that help?"

The boy brightened. "Sure, Daddy."

"Good. Now, go find your brothers and tell them I'm in the mood to play catch. I'll meet everyone in the backyard in ten minutes."

"Yippee!"

When he was alone with his wife in the kitchen, he took her in his arms, buried his face in her hair, and groaned. "That was awful. I want one more year. I want this Christmas."

"I do, too. You did a great job, Daddy."

"Do you think so?"

"I do. I want one more Christmas, too. I can't wait to see what you come up with for your proof."

He shrugged. He'd need to think of something fun. Get the older boys involved somehow. Make it a family project.

He pressed a firm, quick kiss against his wife's mouth, then said, "It makes me sad. John is our youngest. Our last to believe in Santa Claus. They're growing up, darlin'. Growing up way too fast."

"I know."

"I just love this part of our lives."

"Me, too," she agreed. "We went so long without being blessed with children, and they've filled our world with joy."

"We're within sniffing distance of the teenage years. I know those years will bring their own joys, but I'll miss having little kids. I'll miss having Santa Claus on Christmas morning."

"I know. But growing up, growing old, is part of life. It's okay to be a little bittersweet about what's gone before, but there's a better way to look at it."

"What's that?"

She cupped his face in her hands and smiled up at him, her gorgeous green eyes warm and loving as she said, "To quote John's favorite philosopher Dr. Seuss: 'Don't cry because it's over. Smile because it happened.'"

Don't cry because it's over. Smile because it happened.

As the echo of the Dr. Seuss quote rang in Branch's head, the vision before him turned misty. "No!" he cried out, reaching for it, trying desperately to grab hold of it and preserve it, even as the images evaporated. Loss pierced his heart, the agonizing pain as fresh as it had been the day his precious Margaret Mary died, fresh as the instant when he'd learned his John had been taken from him.

Don't cry because it's over. Smile because it happened.

The white-leather-clad woman on the Gold Wing eyed him and said, "Well, Mr. Grinch? 'What if Christmas, he thought, doesn't come from a store. What if Christmas, perhaps, means a little bit more.'"

His emotions churning, he shot her an angry glare. "Would you please keep your fiction straight? Is this Dr. Seuss or is it Charles Dickens?"

The blasted woman laughed aloud, gunned her engine, and in an instant, Branch found himself back astride her motorcycle. As they sped off down the street and across time, the echo of his wife's words remained with him.

Don't cry because it's over. Smile because it happened.

A heartbeat later, the scenery changed. Branch recognized the surroundings. They were out at Possum Kingdom Lake approaching the marina where Luke and Maddie kept their new cruiser, the *Miss Behavin' III*.

The world was back in order, with buildings, trees and everything the way he remembered them when he visited last August. The *Miss Behavin' III* floated in her slip and, to his surprise, the cabin lights glowed. Strange. Why would anyone be aboard this time of night, this time of year? It wasn't exactly boating weather. Fishing, either. But when he looked closer, he saw a shadowy figure at the stern casting a line into the water.

"That's Luke," he said.

"Maddie is with him." The woman switched off the engine and they both dismounted.

"The question is…what are *we* doing here?"

"We're here to observe."

Branch took a step backward as another thought occurred to him. "My son sometimes uses his boat as a romantic get-away spot. I don't think we should intrude."

She flashed another smile toward him and again warmth washed through Branch. *Wow. That smile of hers is better than a shot of Kentucky sour mash.*

"Unfortunately for them, Luke and Maddie aren't indulging in love play tonight," she said. "Come, Branch. Listen."

At that, Branch found himself seated on the deck railing aboard the *Miss Behavin' III,* the stranger perched beside him. Luke stood three feet away but showed no sign of noticing that his old man had come to visit.

Okay, so maybe this was an *It's a Wonderful Life,* George Bailey dream. "Are you sure your name isn't Clarence?" he asked her.

Her church bell laughter sounded again. Luke didn't appear to hear that, either.

Maddie came out from the cabin carrying two glasses of red wine. She set one on the table beside Luke, then leaned against the railing and asked, "What are you thinking about?"

A wry smile touched Luke's lips as he let the fishing lure fly. "Christmas, when I was nine. It was so great, Red."

"Tell me about it."

Luke's grin turned wistful. He slowly cranked the fishing reel and pulled his line in. "John still believed in Santa. One of the neighborhood kids had told him Santa wasn't real, so Dad came up with this elaborate plan to prove to him that Santa existed, and he enlisted the rest of the family's help. Mom sewed together a pair of Santa pants that were fancier than any costume you could buy in Brazos Bend, and my dad tracked down the perfect pair of black boots. Matt manned the jingle bells. Mark manned the pulley. Christmas Eve–actually early Christmas morning–I woke John up and we tiptoed downstairs and caught ol' Kris Kringle going up the chimney. My mom and dad showed up on cue and Branch snapped a picture. John took it school and proved to the entire Kindergarten class that Santa really did exist."

"That's funny," Maddie said. "I can easily imagine Branch doing something like that."

"John was the hero of Fain Elementary– at least until the next year when that snotty Rhonda Wilson tricked her mother into spilling the beans in front of the cub scouts."

Maddie sipped her wine and sighed wistfully. "I'm jealous. We never had Santa Claus at our house, not even before my mother died. Savannah didn't believe in lying to children and Blade wouldn't tell her no for anything."

"You never had Santa? You never told me that before." Luke set down his fishing pole. He reached out, clasped her hand, and brought it to his mouth to press a kiss against her palm. "I'm sorry, Red. No wonder you've worked so hard to make Christmas special for our girls."

She shrugged. "I've worked to make Christmas special for all of us."

A touch of bitterness entered Luke's tone. "For all the good that will do us this year."

"Now, Luke."

He raked his fingers through his hair. "I'm just so angry at Branch. There, I said it. My father is dying and I'm mad enough to spit nails at him. What does that make me?"

"Human?" his wife suggested and handed him his wine. "It's easy for you to be angry at your father. After all, you've had an inordinate amount of practice at it."

"Isn't that the truth?" Luke released a heavy sigh. "Dad has lost a lot. I'll give him that. I know how much it hurts because it hurts me, too. But good things have happened in his life these past few years. Don't they count? My brothers and I reconciled with him. He has daughters-in-law and grandchildren who adore him. Instead of focusing on who is missing, why can't he focus on who is here?"

"It's a disappointment, that's for sure."

On his invisible perch, Branch frowned.

"I should have called him on the whole cancel Christmas thing when he started it," Luke continued. "It was stupid and childish and little more than a temper tantrum. We tiptoed around it for too long because we knew what was behind it."

"He doesn't think we'll ever find John."

Luke turned away from his wife and stared out over the lake, his posture stiff and forbidding. A long minute of silence dragged out and gave Branch the impression that they hadn't discussed John or his whereabouts in quite some time.

Finally, Luke said, "Yes, he lost faith that we'd ever find John."

Maddie set down her wine glass and stepped forward, wrapping her arms around her husband. "And what about you, Luke? Have you lost your faith, too?"

This time his silence lasted twice as long, but when he spoke, his voice rang with conviction. "No, I haven't. It might be hanging on by a thread, but I have to believe that someday my little brother will come home. And you know what? That's precisely why I thought it was so important to put up the Wonderland. It's a Callahan family tradition. We didn't have many of those after Mom died, but Branch did continue the Wonderland. He said it was a tribute to her because she loved it so much, and that he knew in his heart that she'd be looking down on it from heaven and smiling."

"That's lovely."

"It stayed with me. All those years I was away from Brazos Bend I found a certain comfort in knowing that every December the front yard at Callahan House was alive with the spirit of Christmas." He slowly shook his head. "Silly, isn't it?"

"Not at all."

A small wave rolled up to the *Misbehavin' III* and splashed against the hull. The boat rocked gently. Luke inhaled a deep breath, then exhaled in a rush. "Must be all-you-can-eat catfish night at Bass Hollow. Sure smells good."

"Are you hungry? We still have two hours before I promised the babysitter we'd be back."

"Nah. I couldn't eat. Unless, you want some?"

"No."

Luke lifted his gaze to the star-filled winter night. "You know, Maddie, if my father dies under these circumstances, we'll never be able to put up the Wonderland display again. Not at Callahan House."

"Why don't we cross that bridge if and when we come to it."

Continuing as if he had not heard her, he added, "Maybe we can donate it to the town. They can put it up at city hall or something next Christmas."

"Stop it. Don't jump the gun, honey. Next Christmas is a long time away. We have to get through this one first."

"No kidding."

Maddie hugged him hard, then rested her head against him, offering him her support. "Luke, you know it's not your fault, right?"

He remained stubbornly silent.

She released him, took a step back, and punched him firmly in the kidneys. "Listen to me, Callahan. You are not responsible for Branch's illness."

"Ow." He grimaced and turned around. "I know, Red. In my head I know, but in my heart..." He shrugged.

"If the worst happens–if we lose Branch, if you never find John–we'll deal with it. Callahans are strong people. Your Christmas Wonderland will survive. Your traditions will survive. You won't be like your father, Luke."

"He lost his faith. He lost hope."

"Yes."

"But, dammit, he didn't lose love! How does the Bible verse go? 'There are three things that last forever: Faith, hope, and love; But the greatest of them is love.' Why did he turn his back on that?"

"I don't know that he turned his back on it," Maddie replied. "I think he's been blinded to it by his pain. Maybe it's time that his pain came to an end."

"I don't want to lose him."

"I know, baby. Neither do I. And who knows, maybe we won't lose him. Maybe he'll rally."

"Maybe." He turned and took her in his arms. "After all, this is Christmas, right? The season of miracles."

"That's right. I believe that miracles do happen."

"Me, too." As Luke dipped his head to kiss her, he murmured, "After all, I have you."

In that instant, Branch found himself back astride the Gold Wing, breezing down the streets of Brazos Bend.

He rubbed his chest where his heart ached. The too-familiar sensation angered him, so he snapped into the motorcycle helmet's microphone. "So what was that all about? The Ghosts of Christmas Present? Was it supposed to be some monumental lesson for me? Are you going to trade in your white leather for black and take me to see my grave next?"

"No, I don't have time for that. Besides, Charles Dickens had it wrong. We don't do it that way. Seeing the future would be cheating."

Something in her voice gave him pause. "Just who are 'we'?"

She waved the question away. Suddenly, they were pulling into the highway rest stop on the road leading out of town. She braked to a stop, switched off the motor, climbed off the bike and removed her helmet. The serious look in her eyes put Branch on guard.

"I've shown you all I intend to show you, Branch Callahan. I hope you've recognized the lessons presented to you tonight. The question before us now is how you will choose to respond. You see, the time has come for you to make your choice."

Warily, Branch asked, "What choice?"

"You have the chance to be part of your sons' lives, part of the lives of their wives and children. Or…" She gestured toward the highway. "You can go."

"Go?" Branch's gaze went from her, to the highway, then back to her again. "Go where?"

"That's not my place to say."

His teeth tugged at his lower lip. "Do you mean that I get to choose between living and dying?"

"You've been choosing to die for some time now, haven't you? Tonight is your last chance to change your mind and live. So what will it be, Branch Callahan? Are you going to stay around for awhile or are you ready to go?"

PART THREE

Matt Callahan set his jaw and braced himself for bad news as he waited for the nurse to complete his father's examination. Branch's breathing was shallow, his complexion pale. He lay as still as death itself.

Lifting his gaze from his father's still form, Matt focused on the nurse, an older woman with lovely blue eyes and a soothing disposition. The tension inside him eased just a little. He couldn't put his finger on why or how, but something about Celeste Blessing simply made him and his brothers feel better.

For that alone he was glad that the kids had gone looking for a miracle and found Celeste Blessing. The fact that she'd given his former boss at the Agency, Jack Davenport, as a reference and Jack had advised Matt to accept her help had made the decision to bring her into Callahan House to help easy—even if she wasn't technically a nurse. She called herself a facilitator of healing. Jack had been more to the point: "She's a miracle worker, Matt. If she's willing to go to Brazos Bend, then you need to let her do it."

Matt watched as she straightened, removed the stethoscope from her ears and tugged the covers back over Branch Callahan's shoulders. She gave his chest a little pat, right over his heart. None too gently, Matt observed. Was she trying to wake it up or something? Unable to remain silent a moment longer, he asked, "Well?"

She offered him a tender, compassionate smile. "I think the time has come for you to gather your family around, Matthew."

"Oh." He lifted his hand and rubbed the back of his neck. "Okay. Yeah. I'll call them."

Matt blew out a heavy breath, then exited his father's bedroom and pulled the door shut behind him. The master suite had been added on to the back of the Callahan House when stairs became too big a problem for Branch, and as Matt took two steps toward the main part of the house, it hit him. His father was dying.

His world started spinning. As he reached for the wall to steady himself, a pair of loving arms wrapped around his waist and steadied him. "You okay, hon?" his wife asked.

"Yeah. No." His arms closed around Torie; he closed his eyes and held her tight. His wife was no bigger than a minute, but she filled up the yawning hole inside him like nothing else. "Ah, babe. He's dying. I thought I was prepared for this, but I'm not."

"I know. I doubt anyone ever is."

His throat grew tight as pressure built behind his eyes. "She told me to call the family."

Torie pulled herself out of his arms and took a step backward. She lifted her arms, took his face in her hands, and stared up at him with watery eyes. "You are a man of great strength, Matt Callahan, and you will get through this. We will get through this. Together, as a family."

He swallowed hard. "I know. I just wish we had a little more time. I wish it wasn't happening now, at Christmas. The kids…."

"The kids will deal," Torie responded. "After all, they're Callahans."

Arm in arm, Matt and Torie walked to the study where Matt tackled the difficult task of summoning his brothers to Callahan House for a death vigil.

Mark was making a diaper run to the drugstore when his cell phone rang. Spying his brother's number, knowing that Matt was on sickbed rotation at Callahan House, his stomach sank to his knees. This wouldn't be good news.

It wasn't.

He made a quick call to Annabelle. They decided she and the kids would meet him at Branch's. At the checkout, he handed his cash over with trembling fingers. Moments later, he climbed inside the cab of his pickup and realized his heart was pounding as if he'd just finished a ten-mile run.

Mark had been angry at Branch for more years than he could remember. He'd resented the way his father had broken up the family after his mother died, and he'd been furious about how Branch reacted when John was shot and kidnapped off the street in Sarajevo. They'd managed to reconcile in recent years, but Mark had never been able to douse the last flickers of resentment in his heart.

He never would have guessed that his father's pending death would hit him this hard.

He said as much to Annabelle when she met him at the curb in front of Callahan House. She replied, "He's your father. You love him. Of course you hate the idea of losing him."

His gaze drifted over the Winter Wonderland displays as he considered the change his father's passing would have on his family and on Brazos Bend. Branch Callahan was an iconic figure. He'd fought in Korea and Vietnam, then had come home to manage his hardscrabble ranch and bring up the oil and gas that pooled beneath it. He'd made a fortune during the boom years and managed not to lose it all when prices crashed. His wife had made sure he tithed to their church and supported worthy causes with his wealth. Recently when Mark took over managing Branch's finances, he'd discovered that his father had kept up his charity work through the years, even through the worst of times when Mom died and when John disappeared.

"For too long I focused on the fact that he wasn't perfect and made horribly stupid decisions. I couldn't recognize his pain because my own blinded me to it. I've wasted a lot of time with him. And now..." Mark's eyes settled on the display featuring the large brown boot of the widow who lived in a shoe rhyme. "Now I mourn that time, those years. I mourn what we could have...what we should have...had."

"I know." Sympathy and concern showed in Annabelle's big brown eyes. "Nothing is going to fill the hole Branch will leave in this family, but you and your brothers do have a treasure that should ease the pain when you're ready."

"What do you mean?"

"His letters. Those boxes and boxes of letters he wrote to each of you. He still writes them, you know. At least, he did before this illness."

"I've never looked at mine."

"I know. You haven't been ready. I think maybe, after this, you will be. Maddie told me Luke has read all of his. She said he said the experience is like having a one-on-one conversation with Branch."

"I dunno, Belle. That could be the ultimate frustration. At least now I can bark back at him when he barks at me."

"Hey, that doesn't have to stop. I cannot imagine Branch Callahan leaving the earthly plain entirely. Maybe God will assign guardian angel duties to him and he'll watch over Tanner or Emma."

Mark winced. "That's making one great big assumption."

"Your father is a poster child of repentance, Mark Callahan." When he shrugged but said nothing more, she added, "I like to think that the good part of what's happening now is that he'll be reunited with his beloved Margaret Mary."

Without warning tears stung Mark's eyes. "I know. And, maybe John, too."

"Maybe John, too."

Needing to change the subject before he broke down and bawled like a baby, Mark said, "What are the kids doing?"

"They're in the home theater room watching Christmas DVDs. I called Chris and he's on his way. He's volunteered to take charge of the family little people today."

Chris was Mark's adult son by his late first wife. A year ago he had taken over management of the family ranch since neither Mark nor either of his brothers had wanted to step into the job. Branch was pleased beyond belief with it. His frequent comment concerning his eldest grandchild—"The boy has cows in his blood"–always sent the younger grandkids into giggling fits. "That's good. The kids love him. Maybe Chris will find a way to keep Christmas from being ruined for the little guys."

"We won't let it be ruined," Annabelle said. "Branch wouldn't want that."

"Then he needs to do his part and stretch this dying thing out. It's Christmas Eve. He needs to give us thirty-six hours at least, preferably forty-eight." With that, Mark grabbed the drugstore sack with diapers and baby wipes from the passenger seat of his truck, shut the door, and held hands with his wife as he walked toward an event he dreaded attending.

"Do I stay or do I go?" Branch Callahan repeated the question asked by the spirit who rode a Gold Wing and wore dangling earrings shaped like angel wings. He rubbed the back of his neck and said it again. "Stay or go."

"Well?" she asked. She pulled a pocket watch from her white leather jacket and, holding it by its chain, swung it back and forth. "Tick tock. Tick tock. We don't have all day, Callahan. I want to make it home for midnight services and I have quite some way to travel."

Branch stood at a crossroads, literally. The way north looked bright, golden and inviting. South, well, he didn't like that reddish glow to the air, and the octagonal road sign posted a few yards from the intersection made that part of the decision easy. White letters against red said: *Stop. Change your ways. You don't want to travel down this road.*

Branch really didn't want to travel south.

East had a roadblock standing in the road. Looking past it, he spied familiar items littering the roadside. Young Johnny's red bike. Little Samantha's baseball glove. Those had to be Torie's red high heels. As the shortest adult member of the Callahan clan, Matt's Victoria endured her fair share of teasing about her lack of stature and, as a result, wore skyscraper heels on a regular basis. Yep, the way east looked cluttered, comfortable and…inaccessible. That left west and north.

Branch yearned for north. He truly did. But the way west stretched open, clean and welcoming. Ready for more. Ready for clutter.

He made up his mind and climbed onto the Honda Gold Wing making a sweeping gesture with his arm. "Go west, young woman."

She smiled beatifically at him. "You made an excellent choice, Branch Callahan…as you will soon see."

The stranger climbed onto the Gold Wing's driver's seat and started the engine. She gunned the motor and popped a wheelie.

An instant later, Branch Callahan was back in bed, thirsty as a mud hen on a tin roof. He opened his eyes and glanced around the room. He didn't see his celestial visitor, but three of his boys were here, along with their wives. Everyone's gaze was on Maddie, who was saying, "…my favorite Christmas. The gifts were over-the-top.

Branch and my dad competed like sixteen-year-old boys to outdo each other. I made them both take back dozens of gifts."

Luke laughed softly. "It was an amazing thing to see: a rock star and a crusty oilman pouting like babies."

Branch's voice emerged in a croak. "I didn't pout like a baby. Blade is the one who got teary-eyed."

Six pairs of eyes whipped around to look at him.

Matt's jaw dropped. Luke's eyes rounded in shock. Mark closed his eyes, dragged a hand down his face, then looked again and said, "Dad?"

"Somebody get me some water.

While their husbands stood gawking, the girls rushed forward. Torie helped Branch sit up. Maddie poured him a glass of water and Annabelle helped him sip it. Eventually, Luke emerged from his stupor and said, "We need to call the doctor."

"Hold on a minute," Branch said, more comfortable now that he'd managed to wet his whistle. "There's no rush for a sawbones. I had the craziest dream...though I wouldn't swear it was a dream and not something...more. I chose to go west and I could see enough of the road to know that the trip will take a bit of time, yet."

"He's delirious," Matt said. "Where's the nurse? Where's Celeste?"

"She left," Torie said. "She said her work here was done, that we didn't need her anymore."

Branch glanced at the window and took note of the darkening sky. "Say, what time is it? After four? One of you needs to haul your butt downstairs and flip the switch for the Winter Wonderland."

"Oh, holy night," Maddie said.

Branch looked at his daughter-in-laws. "Are we going to the early service tonight or were you planning to take the kids to midnight mass? If we're going to early service, I need to get moving. I feel like I haven't had a shower in a week."

"Sweet little baby in a manger," Annabelle breathed.

Torie laughed, "Well, Santa Claus, you are driving this sleigh, and it appears that Christmas has come early to Callahan House this year. I say we do whatever you want to do—as long as you let the doctor take a look at you first. I'll call him."

"I don't believe this," Matt said. "They said you were dying. You hadn't had water in days."

"Which is why I'm still dry as Moses in the middle of the Red Sea." Branch smiled gently at his firstborn. "Look, Matthew, to quote a great philosopher, 'Sometimes the questions are complicated and the answers are simple.' That's the case here."

"Branch can quote a philosopher?" Luke murmured, amazement in his voice.

The women—all mothers of young children—replied, "Dr. Seuss."

"So what's the simple answer, Dad?" Mark asked.

Branch closed his eyes and savored the word he had not heard from Mark in forever. Dad. "The simple answer is faith, my children. You must have faith. You have to believe. Only then do real miracles happen."

A Callahan Carol

Downstairs, just as Rudolph, Hermey, and Yukon Cornelius arrived at the Island of Misfit Toys, Chris Callahan heard the front doorbell ring. "I'll get it," Johnny said, scrambling to his feet. "This song drives me crazy."

Aware that this was a delicate time for the family, Chris rose and followed his young cousin. Dad and his brothers wouldn't want to entertain visitors right now. He'd play gatekeeper.

By the time he reached the entryway, Johnny had the door open. Chris heard a stranger ask, "Hello. I'm looking for the Callahan family. Branch does still live here, doesn't he? Since the Winter Wonderland is dark, I'm wondering… um."

"This is my Granddad Branch's house," Johnny said. "He still lives here, but he's sick. I'm Johnny Callahan. Who are you?"

"He's sick?" the stranger asked.

Chris stepped up to the doorway. He went to flip on the porch light but accidentally hit the switch that lit up the Wonderland. Staring past the stranger, he saw a SUV parked at the curb. More people were inside.

The visitor was staring at him, a faint smile on his lips. "Whose son are you?"

Chris frowned. "I'm sorry, Mister. This isn't a good time. My grandfather isn't doing well. In fact, he's dying and we don't—"

"Branch is dying?" All signs of amusement on the man's face melted away. He stepped past Chris and into the hallway. "Where is he? Upstairs?"

"Hey, wait a minute, mister. You can't—"

"I can." Troubled green eyes fixed on Chris. "I have to. He's my father."

"Excuse me?" Chris asked, just as Maddie, Torie, and Annabelle entered the room, emotion he couldn't quite read shining in their eyes.

"I'm Gabe." The man winced, shook his head. "John. I'm John. John Gabriel Callahan. Where is my dad?"

For some weird reason, Luke Callahan was having a Grinch moment. He felt his heart had grown three sizes in a single day. He was pretty sure that any minute he'd start bawling like a baby. He turned his head to blink away the tears and noticed that the Winter Wonderland was ablaze.

A soft knock sounded on the door, then a man stepped into the room. A stranger. But not a stranger.

The man's gaze zoomed in on Branch. Luke's stomach took a funny flop. *I knew it.* He heard the whisper-soft echo in his mind. *You kept the faith.*

Mark saw the stranger enter the room. At first he thought that a new doctor must have arrived. Then he took a second look…and the world as he knew it ground to a halt. The flicker of emotion in his heart that had never quite died flared and a voice whispered in his ear. *You never lost hope.*

Matt took one look at the man and everything inside him froze. He blinked, then gasped as his heart swelled and overflowed, flushing his entire body with warmth and joy. A soft, but certain knowledge floated through his thoughts. *Love can work miracles.*

"You're not dead," said the man with unfamiliar features.

But he has his mother's eyes.

Tears welled from deep in Branch's heart...from in his soul...and overflowed. "You're not dead, either."

John. His lost son. He'd come home. *Margaret Mary, do you see this? Our Johnny has come home!*

Branch's heart lifted. "Praise the Lord, it's a miracle. A Christmas miracle." He clapped his hands in joy. "It's you, isn't it?"

Luke's voice cracked as he asked, "John?"

At the same moment, Mark exclaimed, "John!"

Matt started to laugh. "It *is* you!"

But the stranger–John–still had a question that demanded an answer. He pointed toward the bed. "He's not dying?"

A Callahan Carol

Luke joined in Matt's laughter and said, "Apparently not."

"Shoot, you're not getting off that easy," Branch responded, his tone gruff but his grin as big as Texas. "C'mere, boy."

John sat on the side of Branch's bed and took his father's hand. A handshake? Branch was having none of that. He threw his arms around his youngest and hugged him hard. "Welcome home, son. Merry Christmas."

"Merry Christmas, Dad. I've missed you." Glancing up, he met each of his brothers' gazes in turn. "I've missed you all."

When Branch finally released John, Matt yanked him up and into a bear hug. Mark repeated the gesture, pounding his youngest brother's back as he did so. Luke grabbed hold of his brother's shoulders and shook him. "I cannot tell you how happy we are to see you, John-boy."

John grinned and in that moment, Branch saw past the changes made by time and perhaps some plastic surgery to the boy who had always been the heart of the Callahan clan. Tears fell from his eyes and he grabbed for a tissue from the box beside the table. As he swiped it across his cheek, movement outside caught his attention and he blinked. Hard. *Whoa.*

If he didn't know better, he'd say he'd just seen an apparition in the sky. Not Santa and his sleigh, but a woman dressed in white riding a motorcycle.

His focus returned to his son when John replied, "Being home, seeing you again, is something I thought would never happen. I've traveled a long, long road to get here."

At that point, Matt cleared his throat. "You know, I'm not one to spit in the face of a miracle, but John, about that long road? What happened to you? Where the hell have you been?"

John drew a deep breath, then exhaled heavily, rubbing the back of his neck. "It's a long story and not a very pretty one at times, certainly not a story for Christmas Eve when I have family downstairs to meet and my own personal miracle waiting out in the car."

"Are you married?" the three Callahan wives asked together.

John held up his left hand and wiggled his fingers. A gold band flashed in the lamplight. Let's see to Christmas and give thanks for our blessings, shall we? Then tomorrow, I'll tell you about the most wondrous place in the world, a little piece of heaven called Eternity Springs.

The End

Dear Readers,

I hope you enjoyed your visit to Brazos Bend! A CALLAHAN CAROL is meant to bridge the gap between my Brazos Bend series and the Eternity Springs series that I'm writing today. The Callahan books—LUKE, MATT, and MARK—are special to my heart, and it's been such a joy to update them and introduce the brothers to new readers.

I'd like to explain the genesis of the new series. My writing career took a bit of turn when I finished Mark's story. My publisher and I parted ways and poor John was left dangling—alive, but unfound. During that time, the business side of publishing wore me down, and I decided I needed a change. I turned off my computer, shut my office door, and took an outside job for the first time in forever, certain that I was through writing and done with publishing fiction.

I enjoyed my time away from the computer. I gardened. I volunteered. I became a Lady-Who-Lunched. I was happy.

But then something happened that I didn't anticipate. About six months after I Quit Writing, stories began whispering through my mind once again.

I tried to ignore them, but characters can be insistent. Nine months after I Quit Writing, encouraged by my husband and writer friends, I began to listen to them. On one of those nights when I simply couldn't sleep, I sneaked back into my office and something magical happened.

I wrote for the sheer joy of writing. I wrote what I wanted to write, not on deadline or to please an editor or honestly, even to please a reader. I wrote without paying one bit of attention to the "rules."

I wrote John Callahan's story, not like I'd originally envisioned it, but in a way that was right for both him and me at that time. You see, John had started over. He even had a new name since he began to go by his middle name, Gabriel.

John (Gabe) and I both had new beginnings.

While contractually, I couldn't publish that book as the fourth book in the series, I did find a new publisher who allowed me to tell the story as the beginning of a new series. ***ANGEL'S REST*** *is John Gabriel Callahan's story, and it's the first book in my Eternity Springs series.*

With ***ANGEL'S REST****, I received my first ever starred review from Publishers Weekly. They named it one of the top 100 books of the year and* *in the winter of 2014, it made the New York Times bestseller list.*

The best thing I ever did for my writing and my career was to Quit. :)

New beginnings.
Welcome to mine.
Welcome to Eternity Springs.

Warmest wishes,
Emily

Read on for an excerpt from

ANGEL'S REST

AN ETERNITY SPRINGS NOVEL

CHAPTER 1

Eagle's Way Estate
Outside of Eternity Springs, Colorado

Holding a 9 mm Glock in one hand and a tumbler of single-malt scotch in the other, John Gabriel Callahan stared out the mountain home's wall of windows and knew it was time to take a hike. An hour ago he'd watched a gray cloud bank roll in and swallow the rocky peaks above. The rain had turned to snow twenty minutes later. Now a thin layer of white dusted the branches of the trees that surrounded him in every direction. Evergreens and aspen—yellow, gold, and orange with autumn. It was a breathtaking view. A lonely beauty.

It was perfect place to…hike.

He set down his glass without sampling the whiskey, then shifted the automatic from his left hand to his right.

He held it balanced on his palm, testing the weight, absorbing its warmth. How long had it been since he'd held a gun? Long enough for it to feel foreign. Not nearly long enough to forget.

Heaven knows he needed to forget.

A bitter smile hovered on his lips. He stuck the Glock into his jeans at the small of his back, and ignoring the jackets hanging on the coat rack, exited the house.

He paused long enough to lock the door behind him and secure the key in the lock box like a good guest should. Then he paused on the wide wooden deck, surveyed the area, and debated which way to go. Up into the mountains behind him? Along the shallow creek that bisected the high, narrow valley? Across the creek to the tree-covered slopes rising before him? It didn't much matter. Wilderness stretched in every direction. The memories traveled with him everywhere.

He chose to climb the mountain behind him, where the path appeared a little rockier, the forest a bit more dense. The more rigorous the path, the better.

He hiked a long time, his thoughts bouncing between events of his life. His lives. That's how he thought of it.

He'd had his life in Texas, then the dark months over-seas and his struggle for survival, and finally the new life when he'd started over. The third time, he'd gotten it right. *The third time's the charm.*

Charmed. Magical.

Over.

A bitter wind whipped around him, and he grew as numb on the outside as he'd been on the inside for the better part of a year now. Weariness weighted his legs and his soul.

The snowfall intensified, visibility decreased. As the ground disappeared beneath a blanket of white, he idly wondered if this snow would last until spring. It was early in the season for snow, so he doubted it. Although, at this high altitude, with this low temperature, who knew? Bet it wasn't more than fifteen degrees. A man could freeze to death.

But that way was too easy.

He turned into the wind, and in the echo of wind and memory he thought he heard a sound.

Listening hard, he heard it again and his gut clenched. It sounded like...laughter. The sweet, familiar notes of laughter. A woman's. A child's. Happy.

Haunted, Gabe closed his eyes and shuddered.

No laughter, just ghosts.

Over. It's over. I'm done. He broke into a jog, chasing the imaginary sound or running from it, he didn't know.

It didn't matter. He moved deeper into the forest, uphill and down, paying scant attention to his path until trees gave way to rolling meadow. It was a beautiful, peaceful place.

Their suburban home in Virginia had been a beautiful, peaceful place. A sanctuary.

The imagined echoes of laughter swelled and strengthened into a whirlwind of memory, sweet and pure, and Gabe listened and yearned until the sound transformed and all he heard were screams. He was so very tired of the screams.

In a Rocky Mountain meadow, Gabe Callahan tripped and fell flat on his face. He lay in the biting cold and snow, breathing as if he'd run a marathon, sweat—or maybe tears—running down his face. He wanted to die. Dear God, he wanted to die. Here. Today. Now.

Right now.

Today would have been Matthew's sixth birthday.

Enough. He climbed to a kneeling position and reached for the Glock. This time the weapon felt natural in his grip. He flicked off the safety and chambered a round. Shutting his eyes, he took one last deep breath. A sense of peace surrounded him like the snowfall, and he was ready.

The force hit him without warning, a hard body blow to the back that knocked him forward and sent the Glock sailing from his grip. Weight settled atop him.

Gabe's thoughts flew like bullets. Not a man. Fur. An animal. Sharp claws dug into his back. Mountain lion?

Would fangs sink into his neck?

Instinct kicked in, and in a strange twist of fate, Gabe prepared to fight for his life. He rolled and the animal rolled with him and let out a sound. Gabe froze. This wasn't a mountain cat.

Arf, arf, arf. It pounced again, its forelegs landing on Gabe's chest, and a long wet tongue rolling out to lick his face.

A dog.

Gabe's breath fogged on the air as he let out a heavy sigh, pushed the dog off his chest, and sat up. It was a goofy, too-friendly, starved-to-skin-and-bones boxer with floppy ears and a crooked tail. Gabe turned his head as the tongue came back and bathed his face in slobber once again.

Then, for the first time in months, John Gabriel Callahan smiled.

"You're an angel, Dr. Nic," said the fifth-grader, her arms full of a shaggy-haired, mixed-breed puppy and her eyes swimming with tears. "I love you. I'm so glad you moved home to Eternity Springs. I knew you'd be able to fix Mamey, and that we wouldn't have to put him down like Daddy said."

Nicole Sullivan stood at the doorway of her veterinary clinic and waved at the girl's mother, Lisa Myers, who waited in the ten-year-old sedan on the street, her eight-month-old son strapped into a car seat in the back. "I'm glad I could help,

Beth. And I'll enjoy your mom's canned peaches all winter long."

The smile remained on her face until the car drove off and she sighed and murmured, "Too bad I can't pay the electric bill in peaches."

Or baked goods. Or venison. She had managed to barter a case of elderberry wine for a radiator hose replacement on her truck.

"Mom says you have to stop giving away your services," said Lori Reese, Nic's volunteer assistant and seventeen-year-old goddaughter.

"Like your mother doesn't let Marilyn Terrell pay for a portion of her groceries with free video rentals," Nic fired back. "Rentals she seldom uses."

Lori shrugged. "My mom is queen of 'Do as I say, not as I do.' "

"That's true." It was also true that Nic had a severe cash-flow problem. In the five years since her divorce, she'd worked hard to pay down the debt her sleazy, tax evading ex had dumped in her lap, but she still had a long way to go. Those bills on top of her school loans and a practice whose invoices were paid in foodstuffs as often as currency made meeting monthly expenses a challenge.

"Let's swab the decks around here, Lori, and call it a day," Nic said, checking her watch. "I have an appointment at the bank, and with any luck, I'll be through in time to catch a bite of supper at the Bristlecone Café before it closes." She still had two free specials coming in payment for suturing the cut on Billy Hawkins' chin after his skateboard accident.

As the closest thing this county of 827 permanent residents had to a medical doctor since Doc Ellis died in August, Nic stitched up almost as many two-legged creatures as four-legged ones these days. While she was glad to help with minor injuries, Eternity was desperate for a doctor.

"Mrs. Hawkins is closing for supper?" Lori pursed her lips in surprise as she grabbed the bottle of disinfectant from the supply closet. "Wow. She never does that. I knew this meeting tonight was a big deal, but…wow."

"It's an important announcement. Eternity Springs needs a miracle."

Lori wrinkled her nose and squirted lemon-scented spray on the exam table. "I don't think building a prison in town qualifies as a miracle."

"I can't honestly say I'm thrilled at the prospect myself, but it would bring jobs to town and boost our permanent population. The town needs that if we're going to survive."

"Tell me about it." Lori tore a handful of paper towels from a roll and went to work. "Even if they're not going on to college, everyone leaves town after high school graduation because the only work here is summer work. Mom says it wasn't like that when you were my age. I want to go away to college and vet school, but I also want to be able to come back home to live after I graduate. I love Eternity Springs."

"I hear you." Nic had fallen in love with the tiny mountain town when she and her mom moved here to be close to Mom's sister and her husband. Nic's jerk of a father—her mom's married lover—had finally cut all ties with his mistress and their daughter. Nic had been nine years old and devastated, and the place and its people had given her a hug and a home. Years later when her marriage fell apart, she could have gone anywhere to rebuild, but this mountain valley had called to her soul.

She'd spent a year at a clinic in Alamosa to reacquaint herself with large-animal veterinary medicine, and then finally she'd come home. She'd renovated her late uncle's dental office into a vet clinic and scraped by.

Nic loved Eternity just as it was, but she recognized that her hometown wouldn't thrive and perhaps not even survive if the local leaders didn't succeed in bringing in some sort of new industry. New jobs meant new residents, which would be good for everyone. A new prison would definitely bring that doctor they needed so desperately to town. If Mayor Hank Townsend relayed a thumbs-up on the prison tonight, she could at least look forward to having that particular burden shifted off her shoulders.

"I don't want to live anywhere else, Lori," she told her young assistant. "If building a prison in the valley means we get to stay here, then I'll help clear the land for it myself."

Lori sighed dramatically, reminding Nic of the teenager's mother at the same age. Those two were so much alike it was scary.

"You're right. I see that." Lori's expression clouded with worry as she met Nic's gaze. "But I love Eternity Springs as it is. What if we do get the prison and it changes us?"

Nic's stomach gave a little twist at the thought, but experience had taught her how to answer Lori's question.

"Change happens whether we like it or not. The trick is to accept it, to make it work for us as best we can. Who knows? Maybe it'll bring that man your mom's been waiting for to town."

Lori rolled her eyes. "Great. I've always wanted a criminal for a stepdad."

"I was thinking more of a tall, dark, and handsome contractor." She waggled her brows and added, "Who wears a tool belt. Sarah has always had a thing for tool belts."

"Dr. Nic, puh-lease! That's my mom you're talking about. Besides, we already have a handful of contractors in town. I can't say I'm impressed."

Nic laughed and carried the trash bag outside, where sometime in the ten minutes since young Beth had left with her Mamey a light snowfall had begun. Years of experience told Nic the flurries wouldn't stick, but this did represent the first snowfall of the season. Winter was bearing down upon Eternity, and Nic recognized the fact with dismay.

Once upon a time, winter had been her favorite season.

Cold weather invigorated her. She loved the holidays, winter sports, and cozy nights snuggling in front of a fire with the man she loved. But a series of really awful winters had all but ruined the season for her. First she'd found her husband in bed with another woman two weeks before Christmas. Then a stroke took her beloved uncle David the following November. The next winter, the financial fallout from an ugly, prolonged divorce took its toll, and Nic was forced to sell her share of her Colorado Springs vet practice. Then, on New Year's Eve of her first winter back in Eternity Springs, her mom and her aunt had dropped the bombshell that they'd bought a condo in Florida and moving day was two weeks away. Now Nic couldn't feel the sting of a snowflake on her cheek without mourning all that she'd lost.

And wondering what losses the coming winter would bring.

Attempting to ward off the melancholy that threatened, she exhaled a cleansing breath and hauled the trash bag outside to the waste cans, which she then rolled out to the street for tomorrow morning's pickup.

When she was halfway back to the clinic, an unfamiliar red Jeep Wrangler skidded to a stop at the curb. Nic's steps slowed as a bedraggled stranger climbed out of the vehicle. He was tall, broad, and trim with dark hair overdue for a cut and a square jaw that needed a shave even worse. He reached into the backseat to reappear with an armful of struggling dog—a skinny brindle boxer whose left hind leg appeared to be bleeding badly.

Nic picked up her step. "Lori? Emergency patient coming." To the man, she called, "Bring him here."

The stranger followed Nic into the clinic. Lori took one look and then set about preparing the supply tray Nic would need. The stranger placed the boxer on the exam table Nic indicated and held him in place.

"What happened?" she asked.

Concern shadowed his whiskey-brown eyes. "A damned leghold trap."

"He's your dog?"

He shook his head. "No. He's probably a stray. Our paths crossed a few days ago while I was hiking the backcountry, but he didn't hang around or follow me home. When I was hiking on Murphy Mountain today I heard something howling in pain, so I tracked the sound and found him caught in the trap."

"You poor baby," she murmured to the dog.

"We tussled a bit when I tried to free him. I'm afraid I made his injuries worse."

Nic sedated the suffering animal and made a cursory examination. Lacerations, trauma where he'd chewed himself. Broken teeth. She studied the bone. "Not fractured, believe it or not. Significant muscle damage, but I think we can save the leg."

With that pronouncement, Nic focused on her patient and went to work.

Gabe breathed a little easier when he saw the competent, methodical manner in which the vet acted. Dr. Nicole Sullivan of Eternity Springs Veterinary Clinic—according to the sign beside the door—obviously knew what she was doing. He could leave with a clear conscience.

Instead, Gabe stayed right where he was, watching the woman work.

One minute stretched to five, then to ten. She had good hands—long, narrow fingers that moved with a surety of purpose. Straight white teeth tugged at a full lower lip when she tied off sutures. He judged her to be younger than he was, but not by a lot. Early thirties, he'd guess. She was petite but shapely, fair-skinned with a dusting of freckles across her nose. She wore her blond hair long and pulled back in a ponytail; plain gold studs were in her ears. He saw no rings on her fingers beneath the latex gloves.

She spoke in a quiet, confident voice as she explained her actions to the teenager. A teacher with her apprentice, he thought. She was good at it, too. Gentle and warm, her tone soothing and compassionate. A healer.

Gabe didn't belong here. He should leave.

Only he didn't want to leave.

"So where did you come from, boy?" the vet asked the unconscious dog as she frowned over something on his belly. "He's little more than a puppy. Judging by his body weight and the state of his coat, he's probably been out in the wild for a while."

"Think he could have been abandoned at birth?" the teenager asked. "No collar on him, and I've never seen a boxer his age who still has his tail. This one is crooked, too. If he had an owner, you'd think they'd have docked his tail."

"It's a cute tail," the vet declared. "Gives him character."

Gabe tugged a worn leather dog collar from his back pocket. "Here. I have his collar. It came loose while I was trying to free him from the trap."

He handed the collar to the teenager, who checked its heart-shaped metal tag. "Rabies vaccine is current from a clinic in Oklahoma. Bet he belonged to summer tourists and got lost from his family."

"I don't recall any lost dog notices for a boxer," the vet said. "We'll make some calls. He could have traveled a long way." She glanced up at Gabe. "Where did you find him?"

"Murphy Mountain."

Surprise lit the vet's pretty blue eyes. "That's private property."

"Not private enough, apparently. The owner didn't set that trap."

The teenager's head jerked around. "How do you know? Are you a Davenport?"

"No."

The girl waited expectantly, and when Gabe remained stubbornly silent, she tried again. "If you know the owner didn't set the trap, then you must be a friend of the Davenports. That, or you're just another trespasser."

Gabe gave in. "Jack Davenport is a friend."

The girl's chin came up. "Then would you give him a message for me? Tell him that I'm looking for his cousin, Cameron Murphy."

"Lori," said the vet, a thread of steel beneath the warmth. "Don't."

"But—"

"Lori Elizabeth, no."

A mutinous expression settled on the girl's face, but she went silent. Gabe tried not to be interested in what that bit of drama had been about. Davenport business, obviously. Definitely none of his.

He needed to leave. Should have just dropped off the dog and hightailed it. Why had he hung around, anyway?

That wasn't like him.

The *beep beep* of a car horn sounded outside. "There's your ride, Lori," said the vet, lifting a gauze bandage roll from the supply tray. "Tell your mom I'll see her at the school tonight, okay?"

The teenager hesitated and darted a glance at Gabe. "I could stay, Dr. Nic."

"Thanks, sweetie, but you go on. I'm going to wrap this bandage and I'll be done here."

The girl didn't like leaving the vet alone with a stranger, and Gabe couldn't blame her. He should speak up. Say he was leaving, too. Instead, for some inexplicable reason, he kept his lips zipped.

Beep beep. "Oh, all right." The girl tugged off her gloves, then looked him straight in the eyes. "What was your name, mister?"

His lips twitched and he acknowledged her challenge with a nod. "Gabe Callahan."

"I'll tell Mom you won't be long," she said, shifting her gaze to the vet. On her way out the door, she paused and added, "By the way, I think Mom is having supper with Sheriff Turner."

In the wake of the girl's departure, Gabe shoved his hands in his jeans pockets and observed, "That was subtle."

"We watch out for one another around here." She quickly and efficiently wrapped the bandage, released the locks on the table where the dog lay, and rolled it toward a wall lined with crates. When she opened the door to a medium-sized wire box, Gabe stepped forward.

"Let me help."

"Thanks."

Careful of the boxer's injured leg, he slipped his hands beneath the dog's torso and shifted him into the crate.

When he stepped back, Dr. Nic was frowning at him.

"What? Did I do it wrong? Did I hurt him?"

"Before, I was concentrating on the dog. I didn't notice." She gestured toward his chest. "That's your blood, not his."

Gabe glanced down at his shirt. "More his than mine, and my fault for being careless. He got me a time or two before I thought enough to use my shirt to wrap his head while I released him from the trap."

"Why didn't you use your coat?"

"Wasn't mine."

He watched her silently mouth a word that just might have been idiot. Gabe almost grinned.

"Scratches or bites?"

"Both."

She sighed heavily. "Go sit on the table and take off your shirt."

"There's no need for that," he said, uneasy over how appealing he found the idea.

"That dog's been running wild. At the very least you need the wounds flushed and examined." She pointed toward the table.

He hesitated, and she scowled at him. "Now."

Gabe gave in to both their desires. He tugged off his shirt and it wasn't until he heard her shocked gasp that he realized just what he'd done. The scars had been a part of him for so long now that he forgot he even had them. He unconsciously straightened, bracing himself against the barrage of questions sure to come. Questions he had no intention of answering. That part of his life was a closed book.

The pretty veterinarian surprised him. But for that one betraying inhalation, her professionalism never slipped. Maybe her gaze was a bit softer, her touch as gentle as the snowfall, but she never once recoiled or eyed him with pity. Gradually Gabe relaxed. For a few stolen moments he allowed himself to pleasure in the sensation of human touch upon his skin.

"I'll quarantine the boxer," she said. "You should drive into Gunnison and see Dr. Hander at the medical clinic. He'll put you on prophylactic antibiotics. When was your last tetanus shot?"

"Last year."

"Good."

Next she ran through a series of basic questions about his medical history, and then asked him to lie on his back. "Your legs will hang off the table, I'm afraid, but this way will keep your pants dry."

His jeans had been wet since he wrestled with the dog, but he kept that detail to himself and studied her through half-closed eyes as she prepared to bathe his wounds with saline. Her beauty was the wholesome, girl-next-door type. He figured the lack of a ring on her finger was due to work-related safety factors rather than marital status. Bet she was married with a couple of kids.

Pain sliced through him as she applied the solution, and Gabe sucked in a breath.

"Sorry," she murmured. "It's important to clean all these scratches."

"Wouldn't want them to scar," he replied, his tone desert dry.

He saw the question in her eyes, and she must have seen the answer in his, because she kept quiet. She moved a step closer and caught a whiff of her scent. Summertime peaches, ripe and juicy. Now there was an incongruous item for a cold autumn day. Her gentle finger brushed across a hard ridge of scar tissue and she softly said, "More than a hundred and thirty bacterial diseases can be transmitted to humans from a dog's mouth, Mr. Callahan. Dr. Hander will tell you what to watch for, but as long as you take the antibiotics he'll prescribe, I doubt you'll have a problem."

"I'll be fine."

She paused and waited for him to meet her stare.

"You're not going to go see Dr. Hander, are you?"

"It's a long drive. Can't you give me antibiotics?"

"I'm a vet."

He held her gaze and said, "Woof woof."

As she rolled her eyes, he pressed, more from curiosity about how she'd react than a desire for drugs. "It's two hours to a hospital from here. I'll bet you have an emergency stash."

"This isn't an emergency."

Her teeth tugged at her lower lip and she looked torn with indecision. His gaze settled on her mouth until Gabe abruptly lost interest in the game. He rolled to a sitting position. "Don't worry, Dr. Sullivan. I'll be just fine. I know. I've had worse."

Her gaze dropped to his chest, and this time he saw a flash of pity she couldn't hide before she finally asked,

"What happened to you?"

He pulled on the bloodied, tattered shirt and ignored the question. He needed to get out of here. "What about the dog? Will he be okay?"

She accepted the dodge with a nod. "He'll be uncomfortable for a while, but he should make a full recovery. I'll keep him quarantined in case he has underlying issues we can't immediately identify."

He slipped his wallet from the pocket of his jeans, removed a few bills, and set them on the counter. "Thanks for your help, Dr. Sullivan."

Without another word, he turned and walked back out into the snow.

He had almost reached his jeep when the clinic door banged open and she came running after him. She held cash and a small orange bottle in her hand. "Wait. These were hundreds. That's way too much."

He refused the bills she pushed his way, but took the bottle. "What's this?"

"You told the truth about no allergies, right?" As he nodded, she scowled and added, "Take two a day until they're gone. You didn't get them from me."

Gabe stared down at the pill bottle. She could get in all kinds of trouble for doing what she'd just done. For all she knew, he could be a DEA agent.

It was a basic human act of kindness, and it sliced through the scar tissue surrounding his heart, sparking a flicker of warmth in a place cold for too long. "Thanks, Doc. You're a lifesaver."

*Emily March invites readers back to
where it all began—Brazos Bend!*

LUKE—THE CALLAHAN BROTHERS

A BRAZOS BEND NOVEL

CHAPTER 1

Maddie Kincaid was in trouble. Again. Trouble caused by a man. Again.

Maybe she should reconsider the convent idea after all.

"There's the sign, Oscar," she said to the fat goldfish swimming in the clear glass fishbowl belted into the minivan's passenger seat to her right. "The Caddo Bayou Marina. We made it."

The goldfish didn't answer, although the way her world had changed in the last twenty-four hours, Maddie wouldn't have been surprised if Oscar had leapt from the water and belted out "The Yellow Rose of Texas."

Approaching the marina entrance, Maddie gently applied the brakes and flicked her left-turn indicator. Since beginning this long, meandering trip to southwestern Louisiana fourteen hours ago, she'd taken extra care to obey all traffic laws.

It wouldn't do to get pulled over by the highway patrol, not when she had four million dollars' worth of an illegal substance stacked between her dry cleaning and a new sponge mop.

Gravel crunched beneath the minivan's tires as she drove across the lot and claimed a spot between a Dodge pickup and a Chevy Suburban. After shifting into park, she took a deep, calming breath and twisted the ignition key. The engine sputtered and then died. In the sudden quiet, Maddie let out a soft, semi-hysterical laugh. *Better it than me.*

She sat without moving for a full minute. Her mouth was dry, her pulse rapid. She needed to use the facilities. "Okay," she murmured. "We made it. We handled the crisis. Got here in one piece. We did good. Now we'll have help."

Help. From the DEA. "I must be out of my ever-lovin' mind."

Maddie opened her car door and stepped outside. The summer morning air was hot, heavy, and thick with moisture. She glanced toward the boat slips, then back at the marina's ship store and restaurant. "I'll be right back," she said to Oscar as she grabbed her purse before shutting the door. Then, noting the heat and imagining boiled goldfish, she reconsidered. Moments later, fishbowl cradled in one arm, purse hanging from the other, she headed for the store and its bathroom.

As she walked toward the building, movement at the gas dock out on the water caught her notice. Three pontoon boats filled with people dressed in swim trunks and brightly colored clothing motored slowly away from the dock. *Must be one of the swamp tours she'd seen advertised on a billboard on the way in*, Maddie surmised. Her gaze drifted over the crowd before it snagged on the man standing at the stern of the trailing boat as he stripped off a sweat-stained T-shirt and tossed it away. He lifted his arm above his head to take a minnow bucket off a hook, and Maddie sucked in a breath.

My, oh my, oh my.

She may be tired, scared, hungry, thirsty, and ready to wet her pants, but abs like those deserved a second look—even if she had sworn off studly men forever.

He wore a battered straw cowboy hat, low-riding Hawaiian-print swim trunks, and grungy deck shoes. Sunglasses hung from a cord around his neck, and a sheen of sweat glistened on his deeply tanned skin. His body looked lean and hard, with long legs and shoulders as broad as the Mississippi.

Yum.

Her appreciative gaze lingered until a good look at his face made her forget about his form. Even from a distance, she could see devastation etched in his expression. Empathy melted through her. Poor man. She wondered what had happened to him.

Then, as if he tangibly felt her gaze, he jerked his stare away from the minnow bucket dangling from his hand and met her gaze head-on. His eyes narrowed, his jaw hardened. He straightened, squared his shoulders, and widened his stance, his aggressive posture a challenge to her for catching him in a private moment.

Whoa. Maddie gave a tentative smile and took a step back. *In another moment, he'd be baring his teeth like a wolf,* she thought.

A wolf in low-riding swim trunks.

"Oh, for crying out loud," she muttered, deliberately turning away, shifting the fishbowl from one arm to the other. What was wrong with her, ogling a bayou boy when she should be looking over her shoulder for drug-dealing killers? Had she totally lost her mind?

Yes, she was afraid so. This was what an overload of stress and lack of sleep did to a girl.

Dismissing the party barges, Maddie redirected her attention toward the ship store. The place appeared deserted. In fact, other than the pontoon boats now disappearing from view, the only signs of life around the entire marina were a pair of big black grackles pecking at the ground near a lidded metal Dumpster.

Cautious in ways she'd never been before, Maddie slowed her steps and took a second look around.

On the murky water of the bayou, dozens of boats floated beneath the shelter of covered docks. Both the gas pump on the water and the one near the cement launch ramp remained unmanned. She spied an open tackle box and two fishing poles propped against a silver propane tank, but the fishermen themselves were nowhere to be found.

Curious. On a Saturday morning, she'd expect the marina to be bustling, especially on a warm, windless day. Apprehensive now, Maddie advanced toward the ship store's door.

A handwritten sign was taped to the glass at eye level. "Closed for funeral," she read aloud. "Reopen at 1:00 p.m."

Well, that explained the quiet, and all the vehicles in the lot probably belonged to the swamp-tour people. It didn't solve her need for a bathroom, however, so Maddie turned toward the boat slips in search of the *Miss Behavin' II*.

The woman she'd come to see lived on a houseboat moored at this marina. It shouldn't be difficult to find. If Terri Winston wasn't aboard, then Maddie would backtrack to the fast food restaurant she'd passed on the interstate. She hoped it didn't come to that. She felt safer here in this out-of-the-way spot than she did in a town or on the highway.

It had occurred to her as she drove through central Texas at three o'clock in the morning that the Brazos Bend police could have issued a

BOLO for her van. From that moment on, she'd lived in fear of seeing the red-and-blue flash of a highway patrol car.

Maddie noted two normal-sized houseboats and one huge houseboat that brought the *Queen Mary* to mind among the twenty or so boats berthed in the slips. Since the mansion-boat didn't seem like something a federal agent would own, she made her way toward the smaller vessels.

The name painted across the stem of the first read *Playtime*. Maddie's stomach knotted with tension as she approached the second. It'd be just her luck for Ms. Winston to have up and moved her boat.

"Bayou Queen," she read aloud, grimacing. She blew out a heavy sigh, then gazed at the floating palace. It had to be eighty feet long, with front and rear decks, outdoor ceiling fans, and a spiral staircase to the roof with its fiberglass flybridge and swim slide. A boat like that would be called *Bellagio* or *Shangri-la*. Not *Miss Behavin'*.

Since she was out of other options, she decided to be thorough. To her shock and relief, the sign hanging from the rear deck of the mansion-boat displayed the words she prayed she'd see.

However, the *Miss Behavin' II* appeared as deserted as the rest of the marina.

"Hello?" Maddie called. "Ms. Winston? Is anybody home?"

She heard nothing but the squeak of a rubber boat fender against the wooden dock in reply.

Maddie grimaced. Where could the agent be this time of day? At the funeral? A quick check of her watch left Maddie moaning. If Terri Winston was at the funeral and the funeral lasted all morning, it didn't bode well for Maddie's bladder.

Her teeth tugged at her lower lip and she groaned aloud. Had she made one more mistake in a long line of them by putting her life in the hands of a stranger based solely on the advice of that meddler Branch Callahan? So what if Branch insisted that Terri Winston was a stand-up woman who'd listen to Maddie's story without immediately snapping on the handcuffs? Recent events suggested that Brazos Bend's leading citizen wasn't as knowledgeable as he claimed.

Branch hadn't known about the drug ring operating right under his nose, had he?

Maddie let out a long, shaky sigh. She may well have made a serious mistake, but what other choice had she had? Despite her vow of self-sufficiency in the wake of the disaster that had been her love life, she'd needed help. When she'd swallowed her pride and reached out to her father, he'd been off indulging in one of his new hobbies—wildlife photography in the Alaskan wilderness. According to his latest assistant—his latest twenty-year-old, starry-eyed bed partner, no doubt—he'd be beyond cell phone reach for another week—an eternity to someone in Maddie's predicament.

A predicament growing more dire by the second. She needed a bathroom *now*. Raising her voice, she tried again. "Hello? Ms. Winston?"

Nothing.

Maddie glanced from the houseboat to her van, then back to the floating manse. It was a long way back to that fast food place. Not a soul was in sight. Even if she tripped an alarm, she'd probably have time to visit the restroom and make herself scarce before anyone showed up to investigate. "Ordinarily I wouldn't think of trespassing," she told Oscar. "But these are no ordinary times."

Besides, Ms. Winston was a woman. She'd understand.

Maddie wiped her sweaty hands on her shorts and then stepped onto the boat and tried the sliding glass door. It slid open easily, and when no alarm sounded, she stuck her head inside, gazing with interest at the luxurious features and furnishings. She hadn't seen a boat this tricked out since she visited her father for a week aboard a Greek tycoon's yacht. "Ms. Winston?" she called. "Terri?"

No response.

Maddie stepped inside. An overstuffed couch and two plump easy chairs faced a plasma TV hanging on a wood-paneled wall finished with crown molding. A wraparound bar separated the main living area from a kitchen complete with granite countertops and a Sub-Zero refrigerator. She spied recessed lighting, brass hardware on the cabinets, and roman shades and padded cornice boards on the windows.

"Wouldn't Daddy love to have one of these," she murmured.

Maddie set Oscar and her purse atop a stylish iron and glass dining table, then made a beeline for the bathroom. With personal business out of the way and fully intending to return to the dock to wait for Terri Winston like a polite uninvited guest, she nevertheless paused when she passed the refrigerator.

She *was* awfully thirsty. Maddie tapped her foot, then sighed. At this point, what was one more sin?

She opened the fridge. Hmm…the agent must have recently visited the grocery store. Lots of meat, cheese, eggs. Looked to be a Paleo dieter except for the three gallons of low-fat milk. She spied a twelve-pack of spring water and a six-pack of imported beer. Maddie reached for the water, but somehow, her hand grabbed the beer.

Boldly, she rummaged through Ms. Winston's galley drawers to find a bottle opener and, after hesitating over a bag of Double Stuf Oreos, grabbed a half-empty package of pretzels from her pantry. She sat at the table, drank her stolen beer, and finished off the bag of pilfered pretzels. When she belched aloud without even trying to smother the sound, Maddie knew she'd lost it.

"Maybe I'm having a heat stroke," she said to Oscar. Or post-traumatic stress syndrome. But it couldn't be that. There was nothing at all "post" about this stress.

Something told her that drug-dealing, crooked-cop murderers wouldn't give up the hunt for her just because she didn't go home last night.

Grabbing her beer, she tossed the empty pretzel bag into a plastic trash can, then walked past one, two, three bedrooms and another bathroom to the front deck. Maddie gazed out at the bayou, where late-morning sunlight strained through the thick green canopy of trees and vines that stretched across the murky water of the swamp. Long strands of Spanish moss dangled from the branches of the live oaks like gray-green tinsel, adding an eerie atmosphere to an already fantastical morning.

"I can't believe I'm in trouble again," she said softly. This time, she hadn't sought it out. This time, she hadn't fallen for a seductive man's line. This time, all she'd done was clean house!

The urge to cry came over her then, but Maddie fiercely fought it back. She'd sworn off crying at the same time she'd sworn off studly men. She was stronger now. She'd survive this.

But as she returned to the kitchen to gather her purse and her pet, despite her best intentions, a pair of big, fat tears overflowed her eyes and slid slowly down her cheeks.

She swayed on her feet, overcome with exhaustion and emotion and the effects of half a bottle of dark ale. Then, channeling her inner Goldilocks, she chose a stateroom, kicked off her sneakers, found an out-of-the-way spot on the floor for Oscar, and crawled into a queen-sized bed.

Luke Callahan set the plastic bottle of mustard on the ship store counter and said, "That ought to do it."

Perched like a heron atop a three-legged stool behind the counter, Marie Gauthier sighed heavily, her frown deepening the lines in skin tanned dark and leathery. "Ah, it be a sad day, *cher,*" she said, ringing up his purchases. "Me, I'll be missing that old coot. I thought the service was fine and fitting."

Luke nodded and cleared his throat. "Terry liked a good party."

"Mais yeah." Marie neatly stacked Luke's groceries in a brown paper bag. "That man, he loved a *fais do-do,* and he loved the bayou. It's the right place for his ashes to rest."

Luke agreed. Spreading Terry Winston's ashes was the single part of this god-awful day that had felt right.

"And now, what about you, *mon ami?* My man, he say you're taking the *Miss Behavin' II* away from Caddo Bayou. Are you leaving us for good? The ladies here, they will be brokenhearted."

"I'll be back." Luke lifted the grocery bag into his arms and offered her the first genuine smile he'd managed in a month. "I'm going fishing for a few weeks. One of my brothers just bought a new thirty-foot Grady-White. I'm meeting him in Lake Charles and we're heading out toward the Keys."

"An extended fishing trip? *Mon Dieu*. My man, he be pea green with envy when he hears that. So, it's true, then? You're trading in your gun and badge for a fishing pole and bait?"

Luke's smile slowly died as the sick sensation in his stomach returned. He'd broken the rules when he went after Terry's killer. He'd resigned before they could fire him.

"Beyond fishing for my supper for the next few weeks, I'm not sure what I'm going to do."

Marie Gauthier reached across the counter and gave Luke's arm a comforting pat. "Ah, it's none of my business, anyway. My Pierre, he always tells me I'm a nosy old woman. You take your time, *mon ami*. These are grievous wounds you've suffered. The bullets, they are bad enough, but losing your partner…That Terry, he was like a father to you. You give yourself time to heal, Luke. You come back to us when you're whole again."

When he was whole again. *Yeah, right.*

Luke tried to put the old woman's words out of his mind as he exited the store and made his way across the parking lot toward the wooden pier and the *Miss Behavin' II*. The day had been a killer, and he was anxious to put it behind him. He wasn't scheduled to meet Matt for two more days, but after the strain of Terry's send-off, Luke wanted some downtime, some time alone. Time to decompress.

The months of constant danger during the undercover assignment in Florida had worn him down. Saying good-bye to Terry Winston had nearly killed him.

He'd held up all right in the heat of the moment. The gunfight in the Miami warehouse, stealing the car, the mad race to the ER while trying to staunch Terry's wounds and his own. He'd even managed when, after fighting for weeks in the hospital, Terry called calf-rope, squeezed Luke's hand, and died.

It was the aftermath that did him in. The reality that Luke's mistake had gotten his partner and friend killed was a devastating burden to bear. He'd gone a little crazy bringing the killers to justice. It cost him his job, but he didn't regret it.

What he regretted was losing control of himself last night when Terry's friends set out to honor his memory in a way the man would have appreciated. Terry's farewell had started at sunset with a party the likes Caddo Bayou hadn't seen in years. Lots of food and drink, music and dancing.

Luke had kept it together until the band played a rendition of Jimmy Buffett's "Lovely Cruise." At that point, he'd sat down on a bench and bawled like a baby.

He'd hit the booze hard after that in a misguided attempt to dull the pain, and the rest of the night remained fuzzy in his memory. The festivities had continued past dawn, culminating in this morning's church service and the trip into the swamp to spread Terry's ashes. The remnants of a hangover still throbbed in Luke's head and the lack of sleep dulled his thinking.

A dog's bark jerked Luke back to the present, and his mouth twisted in a hint of a grin as the stray mutt who'd adopted him during the past week came bounding toward him from the woods where he'd been off exploring. A mix of golden retriever, boxer, and who-knew-what-else, the dog must have been dumped on the highway by an uncaring owner. The mutt had made his way to the marina the same day Luke returned to Caddo Bayou.

Luke had tossed the dog a bite of his burger, and from that moment on, the mutt considered himself Luke's. Luke took longer to come around to the idea, but finally, last night, he'd sealed the deal by giving the dog a name.

"Whoa, there, Knucklehead," Luke said as the dog went up on his hind legs, planted his front paws on Luke's shirt, and licked his face. Luke pushed the mutt off him, saying, "The slobber factor is getting out of hand. If you're going on this trip with me, you're gonna have to get some control."

His tail wagged, his tongue dangled out one side of his mouth, and he looked so stupidly friendly that Luke let out a laugh. He reached down and scratched the pooch behind the ears before continuing toward the *Miss Behavin' II*. The dog bounded aboard ahead of Luke, then waited at the door for Luke to let him inside. Like a flash, he disappeared toward the starboard stateroom where he'd claimed the queen-sized bed for his own.

As Luke stowed the last of his supplies for the upcoming fishing trip, he wondered why he'd been a sucker for the mangy hound. He hadn't had a pet in seventeen years. A man in Luke's business had no business owning a dog. Since his job was eighty-five percent travel, he couldn't properly care for a pet.

"Well, that's not a problem anymore, is it?" Luke slammed the cabinet shut with more force than necessary. He didn't want to think about the job. He didn't want to think about what he was supposed to do with the rest of his life. He hadn't felt this lost since the day his father booted his butt out of Brazos Bend.

Well, he didn't have to think about any of that now. For the next three weeks, he'd think of nothing more serious than which bait to attach to his line. Old Marie Gauthier was right. He needed time. He'd give himself time. That's exactly what Terry would have told him to do.

Up at the flybridge helm, Luke fired up the twin Mercruiser three-liter sterndrives, then he struck the lines and pulled away from the Caddo Bayou Marina, headed on a southerly course. He knew his way without consulting a map. He and Terry had made this trip dozens of times over the years, first with the smaller *Miss Behavin' I,* then after their dot-com windfall, aboard this boat. This was the first time Luke had made it alone.

Well, alone but for a mutt named Knucklehead.

Luke cruised for hours before the lack of sleep caught up with him. After guiding the boat into a protected inlet, he sank the anchors, then sought his bed. The hum of the air conditioner drowned out the songs of Mississippi kites and cardinals drifting on the air, and Luke Callahan drifted off to sleep.

He dreamed of a bikini-clad redhead playing topless beach volleyball and awoke to a bloodcurdling scream.

Don't miss these other contemporary romances by Emily March

Brazos Bend
THE CALLAHAN BROTHERS—LUKE
THE CALLAHAN BROTHERS—MATT
THE CALLAHAN BROTHERS—MARK
A CALLAHAN CAROL Christmas novella
MY BIG OLD TEXAS HEARTACHE
THE LAST BACHELOR IN TEXAS

Women's fiction
SEASON OF SISTERS

The Eternity Springs series in order
ANGEL'S REST
HUMMINGBIRD LAKE
HEARTACHE FALLS
MISTLETOE MINE: An Eternity Springs Christmas novella
LOVERS LEAP
NIGHTINGALE WAY
REFLECTION POINT
MIRACLE ROAD
DREAMWEAVER TRAIL
TEARDROP LANE

For a complete list of all of Emily's books visit her website at www.emilymarch.com.

ABOUT EMILY

Emily March is the *New York Times, Publishers Weekly,* and *USA Today* bestselling author of over thirty books including the heartwarming, critically acclaimed Eternity Springs romantic women's fiction series.

The first book in the series, ANGEL'S REST, was named a Top 100 Book of 2011 by *Publishers Weekly*. It, along with the second and third books of the series, HUMMINGBIRD LAKE and HEARTACHE FALLS, each earned coveted starred reviews from *Publishers Weekly*.

Emily has written novels, novellas and short stories in a variety of sub-genres including historical romance, contemporary romance, romantic suspense, and women's fiction.

She is a three-time finalist for Romance Writers of America's prestigious RITA award and her historical romance, THE WEDDING RANSOM, received RWA's Top Ten Favorite Books of the Year award. She is a recipient of

Romantic Times magazine's Career Achievement Award and its Reviewer's Choice award. In 2009, the American Library Association named her romantic suspense novel, ALWAYS LOOK TWICE (now being published as MARK—THE CALLAHAN BROTHERS) as one of the top ten romances of the year.

A graduate of Texas A&M University, Emily is an avid fan of Aggie sports and her recipe for jalapeño relish has made her a tailgating legend.

Made in United States
North Haven, CT
20 October 2024

59199628R00081